# STAR GAZER, THE HORSE WHO LOVED HISTORY

*Johanna J Smith, MA, LPC*

ISBN: 1500599336
ISBN 13: 9781500599331
Library of Congress Control Number: 2014913040
CreateSpace Independent Publishing Platform
North Charleston, South Carolina

*Dedicated To:*

*Dennis L. Kennedy, PhD*

# MISSION STATEMENT

The mission of the Star Gazer series is to introduce children to the idea of world peace.

# ACKNOWLEDGEMENTS

Editor—Megan Massaro, Harwich, Massachusetts

Junior editors—Rayelin Grace Hammond and Luke Hammond, Columbus, Georgia

Senior Technical Advisor—Ignatius Joseph Grasso, Downingtown, Pennsylvania

Author's photograph—Frank Byrd, Philadelphia, Pennsylvania

Readers—Mary Bronski, Carol Dixon, Janet Patterson, Lynda Atkins, Kara Hammond, Fran Johnson.

The following schools assisted in the development of *Star Gazer: The Horse Who Loved History*:

Blue Bell Elementary School, Blue Bell, Pennsylvania—Principal, Mrs. Fagan; Fifth grade teacher, Jean McMahon; and second grade teacher, Dana Klein.

Blaine Elementary School, Philadelphia, Pennsylvania—Second grade teacher, Alyssa Boyer.

Perelman Jewish Day School, Wynnewood, Pennsylvania—Fifth grade teacher, Rachel Rosenzweig.

# CHAPTER 1
# STAR GAZER'S FIRST JOB

*Crack!* The stinging leather whip hit Star Gazer's back. *Crack, crack!* It slapped him harder and harder, biting into his tender flesh.

"Faster! Go faster!" shouted Clancy, the driver of his sulky.

A small, nervous man, Clancy was usually soft-spoken and kind. But today, dressed in lavender and turquoise racing silks, he was very anxious and impatient. Star Gazer tried to trot faster, but he just couldn't do it. All the other racehorses in the race flew past him, and when the contest was over, he barely managed to stumble back to the barn. There, Clancy pulled his horse's sweaty harness off, and in stormed Barry, Star Gazer's scarlet-faced owner.

Barry was furious. He tore at the pockets of his green plaid suit and yelled at Clancy, spittle forming in the corners of his turned-down mouth.

"Star Gazer finished last," seethed Barry. "You told me he did well in training and could win this race. I should fire you. I gambled a lot of money on him, and I lost it all! That's it—I am going to sell him."

Clancy pleaded, "Not yet, boss. Star Gazer is still young and learning. His sire, Star's Pride, was a fast racehorse and won people lots of money. Give him a chance—I know he'll do better."

Star Gazer pleaded, "Please don't sell me Barry. I'll try harder in the next race."

Barry and Clancy yelled, "Stop talking, Star Gazer."

Star Gazer listened, ears twitching and tail swishing. Even though he didn't win, he was tired; he needed rest and food. Bugle, the menacing black horse in the next stall, taunted him.

"You're a loser. You can't trot as fast as I can."

Star Gazer pretended not to hear him. He wished one of the stable boys would come to bring him some hay, then maybe brush him or pat his nose. The stable boys liked him. He was friendly, and did not bite or kick like some of the other horses. But today no one came.

Across the stable yard, a crowd of cheering people clustered around Shadow Dancer, the sleek, gray horse who won the race. They fed him lumps of sugar and bragged how special he was. Star Gazer had never won a race—he never even came close. He wondered what it would be like to come in first. He remembered when Clancy, his trainer, first taught him to pull a sulky.

That day had dawned bright and sunny. Clancy came to Star Gazer's stall and put a bridle on his head. Then the trainer placed the harness on the horse. It tickled, and Star Gazer giggled at the unfamiliar sensation. After this, Clancy led him around the track, softly encouraging him.

The black dirt, soft as a pillow against the bottom of his hooves, felt springy to Star Gazer. He watched the other horses trot along pulling their sulkies, and he whinnied hello to them as they passed by. Not all the trotters were as friendly as he was, however, and many simply ignored him.

After that, Star Gazer trotted on the track every day. The track was usually filled with horses practicing for the upcoming race, and he learned all their names. He would whinny hello to everyone and say, "Beautiful day today. You couldn't ask for better weather."

One day Clancy harnessed him to the sulky and stated, "Today is the day. You are going to be in a race. I want you to trot fast."

Star Gazer reared up with so much excitement, that his front hooves waved in the air.

All the horses pranced to the starting gate, and then the race began. From the start, Star Gazer lagged behind the other horses. He just could not keep up, no matter how hard he tried. The hooves of the horses in front of him flung rocks and dirt that stung his face. Star Gazer finished last.

Poor Star Gazer! He felt humiliated in front of the other horses. They snickered about how slow he trotted, and after his loss, Star Gazer did not want to practice every day. During training sessions, other horses passed him on the track and sneered, "Slowpoke."

Star Gazer hung his head in shame when this happened.

He understood that the winning horses received more attention: people visited their stalls, snapped pictures of them, and patted them and gave them lumps of sugar, or sweet carrots, or a juicy red apple to eat. Star Gazer had never eaten a lump of sugar, or a sweet carrot, or a juicy red apple, but he heard that these tasted better than oats or hay, and he longed to find out for himself.

Star Gazer trained on the track for months to prepare for his next race. Clancy made him go fast, then slow, then fast, then slow. Salty sweat and white lather covered him by the end of these workouts. Over time, his shoulders and haunches bulged with muscles, and he could trot for hours without feeling tired. He became so strong he didn't even feel Clancy and the sulky behind him while on the track.

One day Barry, his ill-tempered owner, came to see him. He inspected Star Gazer as if he were a used car he might buy for junk parts; Barry never even patted Star Gazer.

Star Gazer was quiet. He knew Barry didn't want to talk to him.

"Is he ready to race?" Barry barked at Clancy.

"Yes, boss. This time he will win and make millions for us. We will never have to work again." Clancy laughed.

"He had better win. If he doesn't, I am going to get rid of him," growled Barry. "Maybe some fool will buy him. If not...well, we'll see."

Star Gazer's ears nervously flicked back and forth. Bugle, munching hay in the next stall, listened as well.

"You always finish last," the black horse scoffed. "If you don't trot fast today, you're in big trouble!"

Star Gazer's heart pounded with fear. He liked his trainer, Clancy, and he didn't want to be sold. Where would he live? Who would be his friends? And what would happen if no one wanted to buy him? His head ached just to think about it.

Clancy got Star Gazer ready and led him out to the track and to the starting line. Other horses, splendidly attired, their nostrils flaring, lined up beside him. A loud bell clanged and the race began. Star Gazer charged into the lead, but very quickly, just as in other races, all the other horses passed him. Soon it was over, and again, he finished last. Now he was truly afraid of what would happen next. Back at the barn, Barry, puffing on a foul-smelling cigar, hollered at Clancy.

"That's it! Get rid of him! Sell him for whatever you can get. I never want to see Star Gazer again."

The next day, a big "FOR SALE" sign stood in front of his stall door, but no one came to see him. Confused and frightened about his future, Star Gazer paced back and forth inside of his stall. Beside him, in the adjoining stall, Bugle gloated.

"Loser! Nobody will ever buy you. No one wants you. You are so slow."

## CHAPTER 2

# STAR GAZER COMES TO PHILADELPHIA

One day Clancy led Star Gazer out of the stall. He learned that Mr. Garcia, a skinny man with a walnut face, wanted to buy him. Mr. Garcia's red flannel shirt had holes in the elbows, and his black shoes were scuffed.

"Well, this is a good-looking bay horse with a star on his head," said Mr. Garcia.

Star Gazer was astonished. No one had ever talked that way about him before. He listened intently.

"Truth is, I don't make much money," Mr. Garcia continued, looking Star Gazer over carefully. "Not sure I can afford him. How much do you want for him?"

"Just take him now! I'll give him to you," replied Clancy. "Get him out of here before his owner shows up and yells at me. I'm in a lot of trouble because of this horse. He finished last in every race so now no one thinks I'm a good trainer. So please, just take him."

Clancy wiped his hands on his dusty trousers, spat on the ground, and then strode away. He didn't even look back or say good-bye to Star Gazer. Star Gazer's head drooped, and his tail flicked with fear and anxiety. He wanted to ask Mr. Garcia where he would live, but he was afraid talking might get him in more trouble.

Mr. Garcia led Star Gazer into a rusty, gray truck and started the engine. Once they got moving, the truck bounced over the many potholes and rocks dotting the road. Hours passed. Where was Star Gazer going? Who was this man who had bought him? When was his next race? Would he lose again? These thoughts paraded through his mind. Nervously, he pawed the floor of the truck.

Finally, the truck slowed down and a sea of honking cars surrounded them. A short time later they stopped, and Star Gazer's new owner led him out of the trailer. Tall, tall buildings loomed over him. Sidewalks were crowded with people he had never seen before. Where were they, and who were all these people? This was all so confusing! Mr. Garcia then hitched him up to a huge carriage. It had four wheels instead of two, and was much larger than a sulky. Star Gazer trembled with fear. How could he go fast pulling such a large, heavy contraption?

A group of people approached them.

"Take a tour of historic Philadelphia," shouted out his new owner. "Best carriage ride in the city!" Four people lined up and climbed inside. Star Gazer pawed the ground and chewed on his bit. He had never pulled this many people before. Was this the start of the race? Where was the racetrack? Mr. Garcia picked up the reins and clucked. Star Gazer reared and bolted down the street as fast as he could go.

"Whoa, whoa! Slow down! Walk, don't trot," yelled Mr. Garcia.

Star Gazer slowed down to a walk feeling very confused. He watched the other horses that pulled gigantic carriages like his, wondering why he didn't see a single sulky anywhere.

After the first ride, he pulled other groups of people. In between rides, Star Gazer talked to neighboring horses and learned he was a carriage horse. Carriage horses walked instead of trotted. Star Gazer asked questions to learn the new rules. At a light, red meant stop and green meant go; this was important to know so he wouldn't be hit by a car. Back at the racetrack he had never seen stop lights, stop signs, or even sidewalks.

Pulling the carriage full of tourists all day was hard work. Star Gazer sweated while he walked, circling the city over and over. When evening came, and he went back to his new barn in Philadelphia, he was very tired. There weren't any horses in the stalls next to him in the barn, and Star Gazer felt lonely. He wished he had a friend. Falling asleep, he looked forward to the next day when he would see the tourists. Yes, the work was difficult, but at least sometimes they patted him.

# CHAPTER 3

# STAR GAZER LEARNS HISTORY

Star Gazer loved to listen. Mr. Garcia told the tourists about the Revolutionary War and how the colonists fought the British and won. The Declaration of Independence was signed in 1776, and the United States became an independent country. The United States decided to have an elected president instead of a king like the British.

"History is important," thought Star Gazer. "If only someone would teach me to read, I'd read books. Then I could be a teacher instead of a carriage horse."

Not all the streets were paved in Philadelphia. Some were constructed out of rough cobblestones like Elfreth's Alley, which made it difficult to pull the carriage. His hooves were often sore, and when it rained, he sometimes slipped on the cold, wet stones.

One day Star Gazer was pulling a newly married couple from Australia in his carriage. The rain pounded a fierce tattoo and the wind blustered around them. Star Gazer could not see the ground in front of him. He lost his footing and crashed to the ground! Mr. Garcia and the couple shrieked. As Star Gazer struggled to right himself, he wished he never had to go to work again. His hot tears mixed with the cold rain and trickled down his nose. He felt so worthless. He hadn't been fast at the track—now he couldn't pull his carriage over the slick, rocky streets.

Just then, a muscular ghost horse appeared and reared in front of him.

"Who are you?" Star Gazer asked in amazement.

"I'm Nelson, George Washington's favorite horse," the ghost answered.

"Who was George Washington?" questioned Star Gazer.

"General Washington led the ragtag colonists to victory over the superior British forces during the American Revolutionary War. He became the first president of the United States. Philadelphia was the first capital of the United States," Nelson neighed with pride.

Lightning flashed across the sky. Kaboom, kaboom! screeched the thunder.

"Nelson, why did you come to see me tonight?" Star Gazer asked, shivering with fear.

"I came tonight because you need courage when you pull your heavy carriage over the rough spots in the road," he explained.

"What is courage?" asked Star Gazer, his wet mane and tail almost touching the ground.

"It means to keep trying even if you are tired or scared. Even when guns and cannons fired around me in battle, I didn't spook and run away," Nelson declared.

"You didn't run away when the cannons fired! Weren't you terrified?"

"Of course I was terrified. But I believed in General Washington. I talked with all the skittish, scared horses that the colonists rode, and I encouraged every one of them," Nelson snorted proudly.

Mr. Garcia lashed Star Gazer with the whip, but even the pain of the whip didn't make him move. His knees throbbed with pain.

"Nelson, I just learned the United States has a president and not a king like England. I don't understand the difference," said Star Gazer.

"Presidents are elected, kings are not. In Europe there are royal families. People born into a royal family automatically become kings, queens, princes, and princesses," explained Nelson.

"Why are elections important?"

"Every citizen has one vote regardless of their social status, which means everyone can influence the government. Our president and congress represent all the people of the United States. The government provides schools, libraries, roads, bridges, and the armed forces," whinnied Nelson.

"Wow! That is a lot. I've never been inside a library, but maybe I can go someday," Star Gazer wished. The wind blew his wet mane and tail away from his drenched body.

"Benjamin Franklin, who lived in Philadelphia, started the first public library. Before that only the rich owned books. Because of the public libraries, anyone can read books at no cost," Nelson explained.

"Free books! Free schools! Free roads!" Star Gazer swished his tail with excitement.

"Well, not really free. The president and Congress pass laws that tax people. Both people and businesses must pay taxes based on how much money they make. This tax money is what the government uses to build schools, roads, and libraries," neighed Nelson. "I learned this by listening to George Washington talk to his soldiers around the campfire."

"Nelson, tomorrow I must pull my carriage over the slippery, rough cobblestone streets. What if I fall again?" moaned Star Gazer.

"I've watched you slide on the cobblestone streets. Push harder with your chest, and your weight against the harness will prevent you from slipping and falling."

Before Star Gazer could thank Nelson, the ghost horse disappeared into the lightning and thunder of the storm.

When Star Gazer came to the cobblestone street the following sunlit day, he pushed harder with his muscular chest. His hooves didn't slip on the uneven stones now. Proudly he arched his neck and tossed his mane.

Tourists came from continents all over the world: Europe, Asia, South America, North America, Australia, and Africa. Some of these sunburned tourists took numerous pictures of Star Gazer in front of Independence Hall, the Constitution Center, and the Liberty Bell.

## CHAPTER 4
# STAR GAZER'S NEW FRIEND

One day Mr. Grasso, a first generation Italian-American riding Comanche, a brown- and white-spotted horse, talked to Mr. Garcia. Star Gazer stood in the shade resting.

"How's Star Gazer working out?" asked the chunky, bald police officer.

"Great!" exclaimed Mr. Garcia. "He is gregarious with the tourists and loves children. He is a fast learner, too."

Star Gazer snorted with pride. Just then Ms. Scattergood, a petite woman dressed in a navy-blue blazer and a pleated skirt strolled up with Gretchen, her blond, blue-eyed, eight-year-old daughter. Gretchen skipped behind her mother.

"Mommy, Mommy, can I pat this horse?" pleaded Gretchen.

Star Gazer lowered his head so the child could stroke him. Happy, he smiled, showing his teeth. This alarmed Ms. Scattergood.

"He won't bite my daughter, will he?" she anxiously queried.

"No mum, Star Gazer is smiling. He has never bitten anyone," Mr. Garcia explained.

"Guess what I saw?" Gretchen said to Star Gazer as she patted him. Star Gazer's ears flicked back and forth. He understood that if people were friendly they didn't mind talking to him.

"I don't know," he whinnied. "Tell me."

"My mother took me to Independence Hall. I'm going to write about it in school to-morrow," Gretchen confided.

"I've never been inside Independence Hall," replied Star Gazer.

"The Constitution and the Declaration of Independence were written there by Benjamin Franklin; John Adams, who became our second president; Thomas Jefferson, who became our third president; and other important colonists. I like history," smiled Gretchen.

"What is the Constitution?" asked Star Gazer, curiously.

"The Constitution is the written laws that all people in the United States follow. Laws are like rules," explained Gretchen.

"I know rules. Stop at stop signs and look both ways before crossing the street," Star Gazer declared. He felt proud because he always followed the rules.

"What is the Declaration of Independence?" asked Star Gazer.

"The Declaration of Independence states that all people are created equal. It doesn't matter what color you are. Everyone is equal under the law, which means everyone must be treated the same," Gretchen expounded.

"Horses come in different colors just like people. Are we equal too?" asked Star Gazer.

"Yes, it doesn't matter if a horse is black, brown, white, or gray. They are all equal under the law."

Star Gazer's ears pricked up. He whinnied excitedly, and he knew this was something very important.

"Gretchen, when I lived at the racetrack all the horses followed the same rules, and now that I am a carriage horse in Philadelphia, I've learned different rules. Rules keep everyone safe, and laws protect us just like rules," Star Gazer said. His intelligence glowed in his eyes.

"You are very intelligent. I wish I could take you to school with me," said Gretchen.

"Gretchen, don't forget to teach Star Gazer about the amendments to the Constitution," reminded Ms. Scattergood, smiling.

"When the founding fathers wrote the Constitution, they knew they couldn't predict what would happen in the future. They couldn't make laws for events that would happen after they died," explained Gretchen.

"TV, radio, and the Internet hadn't been invented when the founding fathers wrote the Constitution. So these men wrote that if a new law needed to be added to the Constitution, it would be called an amendment," expounded Ms. Scattergood.

"Gretchen, will you teach me to read?" pleaded Star Gazer. "The tourists read newspapers and talk about countries all over the world. I want to understand everything I hear people talk about."

"I'll come every day right after school with my books. I can teach you to read, but I don't know if I can teach you to write. How could you hold a pencil?"

"Maybe I could hold it with my teeth," suggested Star Gazer.

Gretchen and her mother waved good-bye as they walked away. Star Gazer whinnied excitedly at Gretchen, his new friend.

"Come back soon, Gretchen," he whinnied. More tourists arrived, and Star Gazer pulled the carriage impatient for tomorrow.

## CHAPTER 5

# STAR GAZER LEARNS TO READ

On Monday, Gretchen, wearing a yellow dress with a matching yellow ribbon in her hair, appeared in the stable after school. Star Gazer eagerly learned the alphabet in one afternoon from Gretchen. She opened her yellow pocketbook, found a lump of sugar, and fed it to him. Gently Star Gazer ate his treat from his best friend's hand. This was better than winning a race. Now he knew what it felt like to be a winner.

"Good-bye, Star Gazer, I'll come back and teach you more," Gretchen promised as she left for the day.

Star Gazer whinnied good-bye. The taste of sugar remained in his heart forever.

Every afternoon, even when it was raining after school, Gretchen came to teach Star Gazer. He liked history and geography the most.

"Gretchen, I hear tourists speaking languages I don't understand."

"These people are from other countries so they have different forms of government, different religions, and different leaders than the United States," explained Gretchen.

"Could you bring history books from the library? I'll read in the morning before I pull the carriage and in the evening after I eat my dinner of oats. I want to teach American history to the tourists. I want them to like the United States," said Star Gazer.

Gretchen laughed. "You sound like an ambassador."

Star Gazer read every book Gretchen brought him no matter how long. He even learned languages: French, Arabic, and Chinese. Now Star Gazer discussed history with the educated tourists in their languages. The tourists and Star Gazer compared different forms of government, like democracy and socialism. These enthusiastic world travelers patted him, and they even mailed postcards to Star Gazer once they returned to their own countries. Gretchen helped Star Gazer decorate the inside of his stall with these brightly colored picture cards.

Every morning in his stall, Star Gazer watched the sun rise in the darkness of the night sky. The golden-red sun reminded him of his mother, who was the same color. It had been such a long time since he last saw her. Lonely, he sighed.

Nelson the ghost horse appeared, nuzzling Star Gazer's neck to comfort him.

"Nelson, why did you come today?" asked a surprised Star Gazer.

"You seem unhappy."

"I miss my mother," explained Star Gazer. "Her name was Tarheel Pride. Her coat was copper chestnut, and she had brown eyes and long lashes."

"Star Gazer, you have a southern accent when you speak. Where are you from?"

"North Carolina," Star Gazer replied.

"The southern states were very important during the Revolutionary War. I think George Washington might have lost the war without some of the great military men of the South, especially General Marion who fought the British in South Carolina."

"My mother told me about General Marion. His horse Ball is my grandfather," explained Star Gazer.

"Ball was your grandfather? It is an honor to know you, sir! All military horses study Ball, his strategies, and his courage. Once, when General Marion knelt at a stream in the swamp drinking water, he didn't see a water moccasin coiled up next to him. Instantly Ball reared up, striking the water moccasin repeatedly with his deadly hooves and killing the poisonous snake. If that snake had bitten General Marion, he would have died," exclaimed Nelson, the ghost horse.

"Mother told me that water moccasin story many times to inspire me to be brave. A malaria-carrying mosquito bit Ball while he slept in the dangerous swamp, and he almost died from that deadly disease. General Marion cried when Ball was sick. He loved his horse," Star Gazer sighed.

As the red sun rose in the sky, it lit up the day.

"General Marion needed Ball. That brave horse galloped at night in the muddy swamps without his rider holding a lantern. Ball was even shot in the leg by the British. After Ball recovered, he remained a military horse. That horse never gave up," Nelson declared proudly.

"My mother taught me that the British wanted to kill General Marion, but they couldn't find him because he disappeared in the swamps in South Carolina. That is why his name is The Swamp Fox," laughed Star Gazer.

"When people study the American Revolution, they learn more about battles in Boston, New York, and Philadelphia. But without great horses like Ball and military leaders like General Marion to wear the British out in the South, George Washington and I might never have gotten a rest during the war," stated Nelson.

"I will teach the tourists more about the American Revolution in the South," said Star Gazer.

Nelson, the ghost horse, whinnied his approval, saluted, and vanished through the stall wall.

# CHAPTER 6
# TOUGH TIMES FOR STAR GAZER

The summer heat gave way to the cooler weather of autumn, and the leaves turned crimson and gold. As the sun moved farther away, the first snow arrived, chasing the tourists from the streets of Philadelphia. Star Gazer and Mr. Garcia waited all day, but not one customer needed a carriage.

Jose, one of the other carriage drivers, told Mr. Garcia, "Don't waste your time. All the tourists are gone. You can't make any money during the winter. Put Star Gazer into the barn and stay home where it is warm and dry," Jose advised.

"I wish I could, but I have too many children to feed. I can't stay home. My parents in South America are poor, and I send them money. After I put Star Gazer in the barn at night, I go to my second job washing dishes in a restaurant," sighed Mr. Garcia.

During the bleak, gray days Star Gazer pulled the only carriage on the street. Snow and sleet covered the streets, causing Star Gazer to slip and fall. Embarrassed, he jumped up hoping no one saw this. Back at the barn, Mr. Garcia picked up Star Gazer's hooves one at a time, and welded metal cleats to his horseshoes.

"You can't slip and fall now. Today when you fell in the snow, I was lucky you didn't pull the carriage over on top of you. I saw a horse and driver injured once because of the icy streets. The carriage slid and knocked the horse down, breaking his legs," Mr. Garcia warned.

While Star Gazer enjoyed his sturdy winter shoes, Gretchen, dressed in a red sweater and gray slacks, bounced in with dictionaries in every language. Star Gazer proudly held up one hoof, and Gretchen examined his metal cleats.

"Star Gazer, your shoes are like football players' shoes. They have cleats so they won't slide and fall down," Gretchen remarked.

"If Star Gazer was ever hurt and couldn't pull my carriage, I wouldn't make any money to feed my children. I have to work and so does my horse. Don't stay too long, he has to rest," growled Mr. Garcia, walking out of the barn. He didn't like working two jobs.

"Star Gazer, my teacher announced the most important world conference will take place in Philadelphia soon. Leaders from every country on every continent are coming here to discuss world peace! The president of the United States is the host," exclaimed Gretchen.

Gretchen patted Star Gazer's nose and fed him half of her peanut butter and strawberry jam sandwich.

"Good-bye Star Gazer. I am going home to do my homework."

The following days were the coldest ever in the history of Philadelphia. Star Gazer shivered in the freezing temperatures, and Mr. Garcia didn't make any money. Pulling the carriage back to the barn, Star Gazer stared into the restaurant windows where people ate dinner. His stomach growled with hunger. He longed for oats mixed with corn and molasses.

Back in the barn, Mr. Garcia explained, "I'm sorry, but because I'm not making any money, I can't feed you oats anymore. I can give you some hay, but that is all." Star Gazer ate the hay, but his stomach hurt from hunger. The wicked wind whistled in between the boards of the barn. He shivered. Even inside the barn, his breath turned frosty.

Day after day, Mr. Garcia tried to find work anywhere in Philadelphia. Star Gazer pulled the carriage in neighborhoods he had never seen before; shabby row houses filled blocks of the city far from the tourist centers. He walked slowly to avoid falling in the numerous potholes in the street.

Suddenly, Star Gazer spotted a school! He galloped toward it and pushed the front door open, but the carriage got stuck.

The tall, thin principal dressed in a brown suit and a green, striped tie ran into the hall.

"Stop! You can't come here," he screamed.

"I want to come to school. I can read and write," Star Gazer pleaded.

"Horses are not allowed in school. Pull your carriage on the street," scolded the irate principal.

Star Gazer's head hung very low. No one ever told him he wasn't allowed in a school. He knew he was smart, and he wanted another career; he didn't want to be merely a carriage horse forever.

Mr. Garcia yelled at him for galloping into a school.

"You are a carriage horse. You will always be a carriage horse. I shouldn't have let Gretchen teach you to read and write."

Finally, Mr. Garcia found a grocery store that paid him to deliver food to customers. He didn't make enough money to feed Star Gazer oats, and the horse started to lose weight. The carriage felt heavier than ever when he delivered groceries.

Star Gazer never saw the customers, and he didn't have any friendly tourists patting him. All day he pulled the carriage from one nondescript house to another. He was so lonely.

One snowy night, Mr. Garcia threw a thin, ragged gray blanket over Star Gazer.

"I'm sorry, Star Gazer. I know you are cold, but I have too many children to feed and not enough money for a thick, warm horse blanket. Maybe the grocer can find more customers for me. But I did keep these mushy, brown apples for you. They are too rotten for my children. You can have them."

As soon as Mr. Garcia poured the overripe apples into the manger, Star Gazer gobbled them down. They were soft, which reminded him of another fruit, the peaches of his youth. That night, hungry and alone and shivering in his stall, Star Gazer dreamed of his mother, Tarheel Pride, and the small peach orchard that grew next to the pasture they lived on when he was a colt.

Leaning against the fence on the large, Southern plantation, his mother and all the horses ate peaches from the ground. His mother's breath smelled of the sweet gold fruit. Her goodnight kisses even tasted sweet.

All the foals chased each other in the pasture under the Carolina-blue sky, and none of these innocent youngsters understood that one day they would be sold, leaving this idyllic pasture behind.

When Star Gazer woke, he remembered his mother telling him, "You descended from a distinguished line of military horses. Perhaps you will carry a great General in battle after you are sold."

"I don't like wars. People shouldn't fight. Horses are wounded in battles. I want to be a veterinarian. I would care for sick horses," explained Star Gazer.

"You have a big heart, just like your dad. Like all my foals, you will bring pride to our family one day," his mother told him.

Star Gazer was glad his mother couldn't see him starving in a stable. Long line of military horses, indeed! He felt like a loser because he lost every race. Not even a carriage horse now! He had been reduced to delivering groceries in the cold. Star Gazer felt ashamed.

Star Gazer tried to push his stall door open. He kicked with his weak legs over and over, but the lock on the stall door wouldn't break. Star Gazer longed to run away, but he didn't know where he would go. If he ran away, he couldn't see his best friend, Gretchen. Only Gretchen and his mother loved him. He didn't think he would ever see his mother, who lived far away in North Carolina, again.

## CHAPTER 7

# CONFERENCE OF WORLD PEACE

M ore snow fell during the night. When Mr. Garcia arrived in the morning, he dragged a red sleigh with three rows of seats from the back of the barn.

He hitched it up to Star Gazer and explained, "Star Gazer, the sleigh slides easily over the snow and ice. I can't afford to lose the few customers we have. There will be lots of people out in Philadelphia today because the International World

Peace Conference started. If the cars can't get through the snow and ice, people will hire us to go from their hotel to the Constitution Center."

The sleigh was easier to pull than the carriage. Now too thin, Star Gazer's ribs protruded. He was not strong anymore. After delivering the groceries, Star Gazer and Mr. Garcia waited in front of The Rittenhouse Hotel, where crowds of people milled around. The tall president with piercing blue eyes strode out the revolving door of this ornate building. Surrounded by secret service men and women in black, he waved at the clusters of people.

"There he is! There he is! There he is!" the crowd shouted, surging forward.

The president crossed the street directly in front of Star Gazer and Mr. Garcia. Suddenly, the president slipped and fell down, hitting his head. He couldn't get up. His private physician, Dr. Kennedy, a gray-haired, distinguished-looking man examined him then shouted, "The president is hurt. Get a car immediately. I must take him to the closest hospital."

Several cars tried to reach the unconscious president. Every car that tried to reach him smashed into other cars or slid into trees because of the ice. Their engines whined, their tires spun on the ice, and their tail pipes billowed foul-smelling, sooty smoke. None of them could reach the president, who lay on the ice not moving. People on the crowded sidewalk cried, "Is the president dead? Someone save our president!"

Ted, a muscular African-American secret service man, called to Mr. Garcia, "Quick, drive your horse and sleigh here."

Star Gazer slid across the ice, dragging the sleigh behind him. The president, covered with a thick blanket by his doctor, did not speak. His eyes were shut, and he was turning blue from the cold. Dr. Kennedy and the secret service men lifted the president onto the sleigh. Then they climbed in too.

"Let's go to Jefferson Hospital. It is the closest," instructed the diligent, determined doctor.

Star Gazer pulled his hardest. He dug into the ice with his cleats and pushed his skinny chest against the harness. This was the heaviest load he had ever pulled.

"Make him go faster!" screamed Ted, who was in charge of all the secret service men.

Mr. Garcia hit Star Gazer with the whip, but as soon as he trotted, he slid and fell down. Immediately, Star Gazer jumped up, but the ice cut his knees, which now bled profusely. His knees hurt, but he continued walking.

Again, Ted shouted to make Star Gazer go faster.

"He can't. The sleigh weighs too much," Mr. Garcia explained.

"Then you get off the sleigh, and I'll drive," Ted commanded. Mr. Garcia jumped off.

Crack! Ted hit Star Gazer with the whip, making him trot.

As Star Gazer trotted, he dug in with all four cleated hooves. The sleigh moved ahead. It started snowing, and the fresh snow covered the broken pavement in the streets. Star Gazer stumbled along trying to avoid the potholes.

One of the secret service men leapt off the sleigh so it weighed less. Falling snow blinded Star Gazer, causing him to fall into an unseen pothole. Barely able to stand up, he was afraid to walk. His bloody knees stained the snow red.

Ted kept whipping him, but Star Gazer's knees hurt too much. He didn't even care about being beaten. He refused to walk while tears froze on his face.

"Stop beating him! He fell hard. I'll look at his knee," commanded Dr. Kennedy. He examined Star Gazer's knees.

"I think his knee is broken. He can't pull the sleigh. Is there another horse around?" asked Dr. Kennedy.

Dr. Kennedy and the secret service men couldn't see Nelson, the ghost horse, when he majestically appeared beside Star Gazer. He nuzzled Star Gazer's neck, comforting him. Nelson pawed some of the snow and ice away that blocked Star Gazer's path. With his warm breath, he blew the snow off Star Gazer's face so he could see.

"Come on! The horses that carried the colonists in the Revolutionary War marched in the snow and ice that fell on Valley Forge," Nelson whinnied.

With Nelson beside him, Star Gazer lunged forward. All his muscles strained. His knees bled. He picked up each hoof, and placed it cautiously on the snow and ice. One hoof, another hoof, then the next hoof. The two horses soldiered on even though the snowy sleet stabbed like needles. The sleigh inched along behind them, with Dr. Kennedy administering CPR to the president.

Star Gazer stopped and shook all over; starvation had weakened him. His pounding heart made him dizzy.

Nelson nuzzled his face again to comfort him. He broke ice with his hooves in front of Star Gazer.

"Come on, my brother!" commanded the military ghost horse.

Star Gazer stared at Nelson. Then he reared up and charged forward.

"Jefferson Hospital is just ahead, Star Gazer," Nelson snorted.

Star Gazer's breath transformed into an icicle, snow accumulated on his head, his bit froze in his mouth, and his eyelashes had ice on them when they arrived in front of the hospital. Nelson reared up and saluted Star Gazer with his right hoof, then gave a military neigh before disappearing into the blizzard. Star Gazer's head hung low, he shook with exhaustion.

Frantic doctors and nurses dashed out of the hospital with a stretcher for the unconscious president. Now Mr. Garcia took the reins, and led Star Gazer home. Cars and trucks were stranded in snow banks. The moonless night covered the icy roads when they found the unlit barn.

Inside the barn, Mr. Garcia brushed the snow off Star Gazer's head and back. Then he washed the blood off his horse's legs, but he didn't have medicine or bandages for the cuts. At last he threw the ragged blanket over the shivering Star Gazer, and fed him some damp hay.

After Mr. Garcia left, Star Gazer ate, but his throat hurt and he could barely swallow. His knees throbbed with pain, and he lay down in the stall. There wasn't much straw, and most of it was wet from the snow. Star Gazer coughed in the night. Thirsty and sick, he couldn't even stand up to go to his water bucket.

The next morning there wasn't any school because of the snow, and Gretchen showed up for her lesson with Star Gazer early.

"Star Gazer, what is wrong?" cried Gretchen, bundled up in a purple scarf, purple hat, and navy wool coat.

In a raspy whisper because his throat hurt, Star Gazer described everything that had happened. Gretchen opened her thermos, pouring Star Gazer a cup of hot cocoa. He drank all of it, but still he shivered with a fever. Gretchen threw dry straw down from the loft and spread it around the stall. Then she straightened out his ragged blanket. Gretchen combed Star Gazer's tangled mane with her hair brush. At last she lay down with Star Gazer, putting her arms around his skinny neck. He felt warmer and loved. Star Gazer nuzzled Gretchen's cheek.

"Thank you, Gretchen," Star Gazer whispered in a raspy voice. His knees hurt, but he understood there wasn't any medicine in the barn. Snuggled against his best friend, Star Gazer fell asleep.

Mr. Garcia found Gretchen and Star Gazer lying in the straw together under the horse's blanket.

"Gretchen, can Star Gazer stand up? He fell down hard yesterday." he frowned.

Both Gretchen and Mr. Garcia helped Star Gazer stand up. He was only able to put weight on three legs.

"I hope his knee isn't broken because I don't have money for a veterinarian. I'll give him his hay, and then I'm going to work. While Star Gazer is this sick, I can't make any money with him. I'm going to deliver the groceries on foot," said Mr. Garcia, who wore three thin sweaters and his only ragged black coat with a black scarf to stay warm.

Gretchen didn't go to school for several days because the blizzard piled snow higher than the cars. Bundled in her warmest clothes, she nursed Star Gazer every day. Ms. Scattergood, her mother, sent cough syrup, Band-Aids, aspirin, and a fluffy pillow for her daughter's best friend.

Star Gazer's cold was better. He didn't cough as much, but his knees hurt too much to stand up.

Gretchen brought her miniature radio with her. Together they listened to the erudite president and other world leaders discuss world peace while she brushed his dull coat. His fur came out in clumps due to malnutrition.

"Do you think we will ever have world peace?" asked Star Gazer.

"We would if everyone had enough to eat, medicine when they get sick, and jobs so parents can take care of their children," Gretchen explained.

Star Gazer understood. He didn't have enough oats to eat, nor did Mr. Garcia have money for a veterinarian. Gretchen helped by putting Band-Aids on her friend's cut knees.

In the afternoon, Mr. Garcia discovered Gretchen and Star Gazer listening to the radio. He examined Star Gazer's knee, but the horse still couldn't put any weight on it. It throbbed, and he began to cry. Mr. Garcia shook his head with disappointment and apprehension.

"Star Gazer, you must pull the sleigh soon. If you can't, I will sell you," his owner scowled.

## CHAPTER 8

# THE NEW AMBASSADOR

Gretchen and Star Gazer both cried. They clung to each other in fear. Neither one noticed the long, black limousine arrive in front of the snow-covered barn.

"Please don't sell me. I'll never see Gretchen again if you do," sobbed the frightened Star Gazer.

"Sell Star Gazer!" exclaimed the limping president dressed in a heavy, black overcoat as he walked into the barn. Dr. Dennis Kennedy and Dr. Esther Feldman, a brilliant veterinarian, followed him. The secret service men strode in carrying gifts.

The concerned and grateful president presented Star Gazer with a wrapped gift stamped with the presidential seal. Star Gazer unwrapped the paper with his teeth. Inside was a thick, royal blue horse blanket trimmed in gold.

"Put this on, Star Gazer," commanded the steely-eyed president.

The secret service threw the blanket over the horse's back. "Star Gazer" was written in gold letters on the blanket. The secret service men carried bags of plump, delicious oats drenched in molasses into the barn. Dr. Feldman examined Star Gazer's cut and bruised knees.

"Gretchen, thank you for writing to me about Star Gazer. When his knee heals, I will honor him with a party at the White House. You and Mr. Garcia are invited too," announced the president.

The president patted Star Gazer's soft nose.

"Thank you for pulling the sleigh to the hospital. None of the cars or trucks could drive through the snow," the president stated.

"Thank you for my warm blanket and the bags of oats." Star Gazer blushed. He was modest.

"I think the world conference was successful, Mr. President," said Gretchen. "Star Gazer and I listened on the radio. All the world leaders agreed that children should have food and medicine and schools.

"Without Star Gazer, I would not have made it to the International World Conference for Peace. But for a second when Star Gazer pulled the sleigh, I thought I saw a ghost horse beside him. However, I don't believe in ghosts." The president laughed.

Star Gazer giggled.

"Mr. President, I have bad news. Star Gazer can't pull a carriage," disclosed Dr. Feldman as she put a cast on his entire leg. "He needs x-rays immediately."

"I need a new carriage horse right away. How will I earn money to feed all my children?" worried Mr. Garcia.

"Don't worry. I'll buy another carriage horse for you," the president reassured him.

"What about me? How will I find a job now that I am disabled?" asked a frightened Star Gazer.

"What else can you do?" inquired the president, who tried to soothe the anxious horse by patting his neck.

"First, I pulled a sulky on the racetrack. But I finished last in every race, and my owner lost money when he gambled on me to win."

"I don't gamble, Star Gazer, people must work, not gamble to make money," the honest president stated.

"My owner sold me to Mr. Garcia. That is how I became a carriage horse. I don't have any other jobs on my resume," Star Gazer sighed.

"Mr. President, I taught Star Gazer to read and write. He loves American history, and because he speaks several languages, he explains our history to the inquisitive tourists. He has gracious southern manners and everyone likes him," Gretchen clarified.

Star Gazer blushed.

The president laughed. "Have Gretchen write your resume. You are too modest."

"Star Gazer and I want to work for world peace. Can you find a job that we can do together?" asked Gretchen.

"I need a new world ambassador. That's it! Star Gazer will be the first horse ambassador for the United States. You will travel to countries around the world in Air Force One," pronounced the president.

All the secret service men clapped.

"What if my knees don't heal and I can't walk? What if I need a wheelchair? You wouldn't hire me if I had to be pushed in a wheelchair," said Star Gazer.

"Of course I'd hire you. Franklin Roosevelt, one of our greatest presidents, had a wheelchair. He couldn't walk either," the president explained.

"All right, even if I can't walk I'll work very hard for world peace," Star Gazer said with determination.

"What ideas do you and Gretchen have for your new position?" asked the president.

"I will help Star Gazer explain the United States to children around the world," said Gretchen.

"I love your ideas. Tell me more," said the president.

"People fight when they don't understand each other. Countries around the world have different histories, different forms of government, and different religions. Just about everyone thinks their way of doing things is the best," said Star Gazer.

"I will write books for children in all countries around the world. I'll teach them what Star Gazer and I learn as we travel to different countries. If children grow up understanding other countries instead of fearing them, we will have world peace," said Gretchen.

"I think this is great! I wish I could go on Air Force One with you," sighed Dr. Kennedy.

"We will take you, Dr. Kennedy. Gretchen could get sick," said Star Gazer.

"Call me Dennis," blushed Dr. Kennedy. He, like Star Gazer, was also modest.

"Star Gazer and Gretchen, listen carefully to people around the world. What do they love about their countries? Teach leaders around the world that the United States is their friend," pronounced the president.

Star Gazer smiled. Gretchen smiled. Dr. Kennedy and the secret service men smiled.

"Take me to the airport. I want to be home for dinner at the White House. Gretchen, call me when Star Gazer can begin his job," instructed the president.

Star Gazer, the first horse ambassador, stood at attention and saluted as the president walked out.

# WRITING PROMPT

Who do you admire in history for their courage?

# STUDY QUESTIONS

1. What is the Declaration of Independence?

2. What is the Constitution?

3. Name three presidents

4. What is an amendment?

5. What is an ambassador?

6. What is democracy?

7.  What is socialism?

8.  Which state is called the Tarheel State?

9.  What is alliteration?

10. What will you do to bring about world peace? Discuss how you resolve a disagreement. (Suggestions: No hitting, don't bully anyone, etc.)

## NEW VOCABULARY—WRITE THE MEANING OF EACH WORD:
## HARNESS

## GAMBLE

PLEADED

SWISHING

MENACING

BRAGGED

# CLUSTERED


# SPRINGY


# LAGGED


# EMBARRASSED

SNICKERED


SNEERED


HAUNCHES


BULGED

PRANCED

CONTRAPTION

GIGANTIC

COBBLESTONES

# COURAGE

# CANNONS

# ENCOIURAGED

# MUSCULAR

# CONTINENTS

# REMIND

# PREDICT

# SHAMEFUL

# IMPATIENT

# CUSTOMERS

# GOBBLED

# DESCENDED

# DISTINGUISHED

# MILITARY

# WOUNDED

# JAGGED

STAIN

EXAMINED

MAJESTIC

ACCUMULATE

SALUTE



BLIZZARD



LIMOUSINE



AMBASSADOR

# ANSWERS FOR VOCABULARY

Made in the USA
Middletown, DE
15 October 2014